For Shar
Best

u. Boulton
7th Sept. 1999.

TAFFY'S WAR

Norman Boulton

MINERVA PRESS
LONDON
MONTREUX LOS ANGELES SYDNEY

ISBN 1 86106 475 6

First Published 1997 by
MINERVA PRESS
195 Knightsbridge
London SW7 1RE

Printed in Great Britain for Minerva Press

TAFFY'S WAR

DIARY OF THE WWII ARMY SERVICE OF NORMAN BOULTON, HAA. GUNNER R.A. – SGT. CIPHER OP. R. SIGNALS

When war began in 1939 I was aged nineteen. I had been recruited to attend a training school in Bristol as a precision fitter. I had been there a few weeks, and not being too keen to live in lodgings, I had decided that I would return home, as it was more than likely that I would be called up for army service. So it was that in the next few months, I was not at work but loafed about, mainly spending my time in the local snooker hall, never having much money to spend. In the April of 1940 I was twenty years old, and I was ordered to go for a medical test at Pontypridd which was eleven miles from my home.

I was classified as B1 grade, which did not mean anything to me at the time, but later I was to consider that my B1 grade was a main factor in my survival; it meant that it was very unlikely that I would be joining the Infantry or be a pilot in the RAF or even the navy.

So it was, a few months later I was told to report on 13th June to Park Hall Camp in Oswestry. My father was working the night shift in one of the local mines. I also had five brothers working in the mines, all older than me. My youngest brother had already joined the merchant navy, and was at Montevideo, when the Graf Spee, the German pocket-battleship was there. He returned home a few days before I left. He was later to join the cruiser H.M.S. Newcastle as a Royal Marine. My father returned home from work on the morning of 13th June and, black from head to foot, came to see me off at the high level station in Aberdare.

I arrived at Park Hall Camp, Oswestry, some time in the afternoon, meeting a lot of other recruits. I was now a soldier in the 340 Battery 95th Regt. HAA and the first couple of days was spent in being issued with uniform and other clothing; we rolled our own clothing up and sent it off home. We were given health checks and also intelligence and aptitude tests. We were to have about three months' training at Oswestry; each soldier was given a particular job to do and some were put to man the 3.7 inch AA guns. Some were put on a predictor machine which calculated the range and height of enemy aircraft. I myself was put as a "spotter" on the Command Post; it was my job to identify all aircraft that approached us, and

I alternated also as a telephonist down in the Command Post dugout.

We had lectures often on aircraft identity by a Sergeant Green who had great difficulty getting his words out and so screwed his face up a lot. I also had a stammer, so I sympathised with him. We had marching drill every afternoon and by night-time we used to feel quite tired. We were about twenty soldiers to a hut, which was quite comfortable, and very soon we got to know our fellow soldiers quite well and choose one's friends. I was called 'Taff' or 'Taffy', which stuck to me for the rest of my army service although there were about fourteen Welsh boys in my unit besides myself.

One chap walked up and down the hut during the night reading hymns out loud. Another always slept with his eyes open. We attended church service every Sunday morning; back home I only went to chapel on the Sunday before the annual trip to the seaside.

We read about the air-raids on London every morning in the newspapers. I had my first experience of guard duty being put on guard on the main Camp gate. It was near the office also, so someone must have seen me walking back and forth with my rifle, and sloping arms and performing other guard drills, because the Guard Commander came out and gave me some practice drill as well as berating me.

I was to learn that because my surname began with the letter B I was at the beginning of the list of names, so for army duties to be done, and there was plenty of them, they just looked down the list and my name was always first; and in six years of service only once was a complaint ever made about it. We continued to have square bashing every day at various times.

I myself had lectures about aircraft and aircraft identification; the gunners had practice on the 3.7 inch guns, with sometimes a Fairey Battle two-seater aircraft flying back and forth to give us target practice.

I had one diversion when I was chosen to escort about four hundred Czech soldiers from Oswestry Station to York by train. We marched from York Station to the racecourse, the people on the way shouting at the Czechs whom they mistook for German prisoners. They were put into a barbed wire compound, so I was patrolling at times on the outside, we slept at night on the floor of the Tote building accompanied by plenty of cockroaches. Back at Park Hall everyone was aware that there could be a German invasion, so every evening we stood at arms near slit trenches that had been built.

I liked sports so I played an occasional game of football. Towards the end of August, we packed our kit-bags to travel to a practice firing camp at a site called

Aberffraw in Anglesey. As usual I was first on guard at the Command Post of the guns along with three other soldiers whose names started with the letters A or B. We were looking out to sea and smiled at each other. We were put in our place by an officer who told us it was not a game, that it was our duty to be watchful on guard as an invasion was possible at any place.

We found Anglesey very lonely with a pub and a few houses here and there. We fired our guns quite a lot, with a plane towing a sleeve or drogue to and fro for us to fire at. We soon packed our bags again and travelled to Manchester to man a gun site there at a place called Chorlton which was not too far from Ringway Airport.

We had a few visits from German aircraft, so we had our first experience of bombing; this was in September 1940. We had one daylight raid by a Dornier aircraft, which flew in and out of the clouds. We only spent a short time at Manchester, and from there we travelled to Coventry, the camp being on a hill overlooking the city, at a place called Gibbet Hill on the Kenilworth road. The Unit that we relieved told us it was like an holiday camp there, with no action at all; the date October 1940. It soon changed after our arrival with frequent night-raids.

Off-duty, we travelled into the town for a look around and a pub visit but as the raids got worse we never spent much time going into the city at night.

We were quartered in wooden huts that were not properly completed with spaces under the hut walls. There was a concrete Command Post with a dugout that had a telephone, and during an air raid if I was on duty, I would be standing on top of the Command Post looking for aircraft, or underneath manning the telephone that warned us of any hostile aircraft that were approaching us, although they could be about a hundred miles away.

In early November we manned the guns from then on every night. Some raids were on Birmingham or other towns that were close to us, and some of the men gave vent to their feelings during a heavy raid, some even sobbing and cringing in the corners of the Command Post. I had my first experience of fright, when one had a pain in the stomach. I was frightened to hell but made sure no one knew it. Apart from the bombs dropping, shrapnel from our own shells used to fall from other guns around the city.

It had been six months since I had joined the army so I was told I was due for a week's leave from the 15th November. On the 14th, a Thursday night, I was off-duty because of my leave that next day. At 6:30 that night the air raid alarm went and soon German aircraft were dropping their bombs. I was in my hut, nervous as hell, and trying to be oblivious to the bombs falling. The raid that night came to be known as the 'Coventry Blitz' and the German code name for it was 'Moonlight Sonata'. Some hours later, myself and one or two others that were in the hut were told to report to the Command Post, as the ammunition that was usually stored in the gun pits had been used up, and we were required to carry it from the ammunition dump to the guns that were about a hundred yards away. The 56-pound shells were two to each metal box which was about three feet long with a handle each end, so it was hard work. I thought it was not a good place to be in an air raid, in and out of an ammunition dump. Looking down on the city we could see it ablaze in the early hours of Friday morning. The raid eased off and there were only a few German aircraft still flying around, but there had been about five hundred German aircraft in the raid, and over a thousand casualties in the city.

It has been stated that the authorities knew in advance of the raid but did nothing because it would have warned the Germans that we had broken their codes, which in fact we had done.

It was beginning to get light when I returned to my hut so it was not worth bothering about any sleep, and got ready to go on leave. A few others were also going on leave, so we began to walk to Coventry Station, no transport being available to us. We could see the extent of the bomb damage as we walked along with a lot of houses and buildings in ruins. We finally reached Coventry

Station and weren't surprised to see that we would not be leaving by train, so the only option was to get a lift to Birmingham. We managed to get to New Street Station where I was told I would have to go to Snow Hill Station to travel to Cardiff and then home.

I had some time to spare before my train was due so wandered into the station buffet for a cup of tea. I sat by two sailors who were smoking at a table – servicemen usually sat among their own kind – and during conversation one of them said to me, "Would you like a Durex?" I thought for a moment, I have not heard of them cigarettes before, so thought it best to say no thanks!

When I arrived in Cardiff I had to catch another train to my home in Aberdare, a distance of just over twenty miles. In the compartment where I sat, people were reading the South Wales Echo newspaper whose front page described the raid on Coventry the night just gone and discussed it. I had no wish to enter into the conversation. I finally arrived at Aberdare, my home town, at seven o'clock in the evening: it had taken me twelve hours to travel from Coventry to my home. When I walked into my home my mother was resting her head on the kitchen table having a nap. She and my father knew about the raid and also knew that I was in Coventry, so they had been very worried, and were very glad to see me.

I had a quiet week, the time usually being spent having a couple of drinks and going to a movie. When I returned to Coventry after my leave the boys told me they had had air raids every night. When I was on telephone duty on the Command Post during daytime there was not a lot of activity, so being fond of painting since my schooldays, when I was always top in Art, I purchased a kiddy's paintbox in the city, and during quiet moments did some water-colour paintings, which some of the boys were asking me to give to them to send home.

Off-duty I played a lot of cards for money, and rarely lost. Very soon no one would play with me; I had played a lot in my teens so you could say I was experienced at cards.

Christmas 1940 came and went and now we were experiencing winter weather. One day in January I was on duty on top of the Command where it was my job to keep my eyes open for enemy air activity. There was light snow about and we had the warning of enemy aircraft. There was very low misty clouds and we could hear the sound of a plane flying around overhead. Then to my surprise I could see an aircraft approaching at only a few hundred feet above ground. I shouted to one of the boys that was manning an old WW1 Lewis gun "Plane!", and in less than a few minutes the plane flew right over my head. I could see the pilot quite clearly. I instinctively ducked as he went over me. I knew he was too low to drop bombs but he could have used his machine gun; the boy on the Lewis gun had managed to let off a few bursts, from the time the plane came out of the clouds and back in couldn't have been much more than five minutes. The plane was a JU88 medium bomber.

I had heard of the Coventry Hippodrome, and one day we were all taken to an afternoon show there. There was bomb damage all round but the Hippodrome had managed to escape serious damage. I was seated a few rows from the front, and one of the acts was a woman singing. I must have been beaming with appreciation because she called me up. I didn't move, but with all the boys shouting at me to go on, I went on stage. She told me to stand behind with my arms around her waist. I must have had my arms too low around her waist because she pulled my arms up and began to sing "If you were the only girl in the world". I had to endure a lot of ribbing back at Camp!

About this time we moved from Gibbet Hill to another AA site on the other side of Coventry, it was called Stoneleigh. It was now spring 1941. On day leave we used to walk about nine miles to Leamington passing through Kenilworth, and one day myself and another soldier named Slagmann, who was Jewish, went to Leamington and thought we would have a cup of tea. We went to the Pump Rooms, which to us was very posh with a small orchestra playing. We ordered tea and sandwiches, we had a small pot of jam with the sandwiches which were so small it would take two to fill your mouth. My friend asked the waiter to ask the orchestra to play *Rhapsody in Blue* but they declined the request.

I was on duty one midday on the Command Post, and we had an 'Enemy Aircraft Approaching' alert. The guns were manned and soon we could see a single aircraft approaching. It was quite visible and the officer in charge shouted to us. 'Spotter', my friend, was nearest, so he looked through the telescope and shouted, "Blenheim Sir!" A few moments later a stick of bombs fell in a field nearby. He received no medals for mistaking a JU88 for a Blenheim, a British aircraft!

Now and then I would be given a few days leave and on two occasions I paid a visit to my brother who was working in Redditch. Later he was in the Royal Fusiliers and had slight injuries at Monte Cassino.

My other brother I visited in London; he also joined up at a later date. It would be another five years before I would see them both again.

I was sent on a couple of weeks' course to Lichfield, the lectures being on aircraft identification. While I was there near the end of my course, I was informed that I would have to report to my unit at Goxhill. 'Where the hell is that?' I thought. No one could tell me, so I went to the nearest station and asked in the ticket office where it was. The man in the office did not know either, so he had to look it up in a book. He told me it was on the east coast in Lincolnshire, south of the Humber.

I arrived on the north side of the Humber late at night so I had to travel by train right around, and eventually arrived at my destination. Never have I seen such a lonely place, with nothing in sight but open countryside. I was glad when in May 1941 we travelled south to Sheringham in Norfolk where we were to have some firing practice on 4.5 inch guns. As usual I was the first to go on guard duty, but on this occasion the corporal in charge of the guard complained to the orderly officer that it was the same people were on guard whenever we moved to a new site. So I was pleased when we were relieved of our guard duty.

What we found queer was that we had bright sunshine but it was very cold being right on the coast. There was some rockets also sited on the cliffs; I had not seen any before. We were warned not to go near the beach because it was heavily mined, apparently some casualties had occurred accidentally.

We moved about quite a lot at this time and eventually, after spending some time in Birmingham, Wolverhampton and Dudley, we travelled to Leeds at the end of 1941. We were billeted in empty houses near Leeds cricket ground, about six of us sleeping on the floor in the downstairs rooms. We had our meals at the cricket ground, and when we returned to the billet we usually nicked some coal to take back to the house with us, it being quite cold. The rumour about was that we were going abroad and I had a job painting signs on Jeeps and other transport. Everyone was inoculated, or in my case vaccinated, which after some days proved to be very painful.

We were all taken to a university one day to have a lecture on physics, what for I don't know. It was mainly about colours. I went out on my own into the city one day, and visited a picture house. I sat in the middle of the back row, all on my own. I noticed a young lady walking down the aisle, and was surprised when she came and sat next to me. I had not had much to do with girls, preferring billiard halls to dance halls, and when someone paid for me to go in Headingly I visited the local greyhound track.

Christmas came and went without any celebration. One day we went to the Headingly cricket ground to get issued with khaki tropical dress and topees which were used in WW1 and possibly Khartoum. They were heavy and cumbersome. We also received shorts which folded at the knee, so one had shorts and long trousers all in one. I painted my name on my kit-bag, being very good at sign-writing. The officers and sergeants had me doing their bags as well. We were told that soon we would be embarking. No one at this time knew where to so we were told that we could have weekend leave.

I reasoned that being a few hundred miles from own town, I would spend most of my time on a train, so I decided to stay, a few others did the same. If I had known how long I would be abroad I would have taken my leave, no matter how short.

Quite a bit of snow was hanging around at that time, as one morning early we were told to carry full kits, and we had to march to Leeds Station to catch a train to Liverpool. I am not sure what the distance was but after a while, not being very robust, I was trailing behind the rest of the column. When I finally reached the station everyone was aboard the train, and the engine was blowing its whistle. There was only one or two besides myself not on the train, and the thought occurred to me 'What if the train leaves me behind?' I finally got on the train out of breath. When we got off the train I could see a big liner which was the 'Monarch of Bermuda' and this was the one I boarded.

She was a luxury liner of 22,000 tons, and usually travelled to the West Indies. The date was February the 13th 1942. I was put into a cabin on B deck with four other boys. I had a comfortable bunk but one of us had to sleep on the floor. The ship's dining room was very big and we also liked the food. There was a shop where we could purchase some of the things we needed. We discovered that our soap was no good because of the salt water so we had to buy some special soap. On the night of the 16th February we left Liverpool bound for Greenock to meet the rest of the convoy.

It was only later that I learned that Singapore had fallen to the Japs. In hindsight I often wondered whether we might have been there if we had gone overseas earlier. Troops were actually disembarking as Singapore fell, and went straight into captivity.

We woke up next morning aware that we were entering the Atlantic, and had no idea what lay ahead of us. After about four days the weather began to get bad and soon became very rough with mountainous seas, and the boys including myself began to get seasick. Some mornings when we paraded a few of the boys would fall out of line and dash to the side of the deck. Whereas the mess deck was full on the first few days, it was now deserted and we mostly stayed in the cabin, moaning and groaning. I don't think I would have made a good sailor! One of the men in my cabin was from County Durham, and unlike myself and the others in the cabin, he never missed a meal. He was rather stout and probably ate more than us, but the weather never affected him. He was one of the boys on watch on the Bridge, and when he returned to the cabin after a meal he would say "Any of you boys like a nice piece of fat bacon or pork?" You can imagine our answer.

The ship was rising and falling rather steeply with huge waves going over the bows, and what was guaranteed to make one sick was to walk down one of the long corridors along each side of the ship, and see it rising and falling and also rolling. The storm must have lasted for about ten days. We were somewhere in the Bay of Biscay, the liner never took a direct course and went out far into the Atlantic to miss the U-boats. Then the weather got finer and we started to get a bit of sunshine, so we were able to have a good look at the convoy. I counted a total of fifteen warships comprising two aircraft carriers, two or four battleships and about ten destroyers and cruisers.

I was on guard one night below deck on the corner of a corridor, and during my two-hour spell I wanted to have a pee. The toilet was near, and I had only been gone a few minutes but when I came out an officer, a colonel, was standing by my post and gave me a telling off and accused me of going into the toilet to have a smoke. I told him I had only gone for a pee, but it made no difference, and I had learnt to say nothing more because I knew I couldn't win.

The convoy changed course, frequently zig-zagging, and the weather was warmer now we were off the coast of west Africa. They had a canvas pool on deck so we were able to have a little dip.

About a fortnight had elapsed since leaving Liverpool. As we sailed into Freetown Harbour some of the escort left us here as we carried on to Durban. We spent about four days in Durban and were transferred to a liberty ship called the 'Empire Pride', one of the ships built quickly by the Americans. The first day ashore, my friend Johnny Gray, who came from Seaburn on the north-east coast, and I wandered around the coloured quarter, but we managed to find the right part of the city next day, where when eating we were surprised at the plentiful supply of fruit on the tables. I remember walking into a kind of park, where a band was playing 'With You In Apple Blossom Time'. We left Durban still unsure where we were actually bound for. We had managed to come through the Atlantic safely and hoped we would do the same in the Indian Ocean.

Compared to the 'Monarch of Bermuda', the 'Empire Pride' was awful. With the ship constantly rolling, sometimes our meals would slither off the tables, and everyone seemed to be bad tempered. We had hammocks to sleep in, some of the men preferring to sleep on deck. After two weeks we sighted land which, in fact, was Bombay, India. It was early April: we had taken eight weeks to get there. We marched from the dock a few miles to a camp called Colaba, the accommodation being a low wall with a square piece of canvas over it. It was very warm and we soon walked about in our vests. Fruit was plentiful and we ate a lot of it.

After a few days we left Colaba and marched to the station. It seemed the British army had no transport. We always had to march to our destination. The Bombay Station was very busy, with the Indian vendors walking along the platform shouting and selling their wares. We had been warned not to buy any drinks because of the risk of cholera, which was always present in India.

It was a long ride from Bombay to Calcutta, which we learned was our destination. We had our first experience of Indian trains when we lay down to sleep stretched out head to foot along the length of the coach. We soon discovered that we would not be able to sleep much, with cockroaches coming out of the corners of the seating. We often had to stop for the engine to take on water, and we soon discovered how to brew tea on train rides. We would try to secure a large empty tin, and when the train stopped one of us would dash up to the engine and the engine-driver would be asked to let off steam into the tin. With the very hot water we were able to brew some tea. There was always plenty of tea leaves available. Some of us read or played cards, or admired the scenery. The line was single tracked, so there were sidings at certain distances where one would wait until a train going the other way passed. About ten or eleven on that evening we stopped at a station called Tatanagar which was in Jamshedpur. Tatanagar was the largest steel works in Asia, and looking from our train we could see the sky lit up and the works ablaze with lights. We had travelled about four hundred miles from Bombay and had about a hundred and fifty miles still to go to Calcutta. While we were at the station we could see some European ladies handing out teas, cakes, and sandwiches. One lady was shouting "Anyone here from Wales?" I got down off the train and told her that I was Welsh from a town called Aberdare in Glamorgan. I was surprised when she told me she had relations who had a shop called 'J.D. Williams' in Aberdare which is still there to this day. She gave me her address and told me to write to her. Her husband was from Gorseinon near Swansea. They had been living in Tatanagar for a number of years, and he was employed at the steel works. I was to meet him in person at a later date. After a while we set off once more, and finally arrived at Howrah Station, the main station in Calcutta. Being on the banks of the Hooghly river, ocean-going ships could travel the eighty miles from the sea up the river to Calcutta. Eighteen months later I was to meet my brother who was aboard the cruiser 'Newcastle' when they docked at Calcutta.

Calcutta was the largest city in India, and was the capital until 1912 when the government moved to Delhi. My birthday was about this time at the end of April. I was twenty-two years old. We got transported to a place called Barrackpore about fifteen miles from Calcutta; it must have been established as a military base for a long time, owing to the nature of the buildings. It also had a hospital and indoor baths, etc. However, we were put into tents or even slept in the open with a mosquito net loosely arranged over us to keep us safe from bites. I could see thousands of fireflies in the dark, and heard the endless noise of bullfrogs. We spent a few weeks under the canvas, and a little black boy offered to clean my shoes and do other little jobs. He must had been about ten years old. I gave him a couple of annas each time. Sixteen annas made up one rupee, the standard currency. Me and my friend had our photo taken by one of the boys who had a camera. I still have the photograph.

We did not like the khaki drill we were issued with and cut the fold-up trousers to make shorts. We were later issued with proper trousers, and wore a sidecap or glengarry. Head-dress had to be worn at all times, and when on guard duty we wore a tin hat.

I had my first day leave so my friend and I decided to go into the city of Calcutta. That first time we had to make our own way in, and an army lorry would pick us up at twelve o'clock midnight. There was a small station called Sealdah nearby where we went to get into the city. The train was quite full of Indians, and they were also hanging on to the outside of the coaches. We got off the train a long way off the city centre, so we had a good walk without a white man in sight. We got to the main road in the city that was called Chowringhee, which was where all the troops went to. There were a few cinemas, notably the Metro and the Lighthouse. These were quite modern with nice bars so one could have a drink before the show. I usually had a gin and lemonade. There was no beer anywhere. Usually you went in late, and if you were on your own you had to be careful not to fall asleep when the lights were put out at the end of the show. When we came out of the cinema it would be late and the pavements were usually full of Indians lying down to sleep the night away. One had to sidestep when walking along the pavement. A few new places opened up on Chowringhee, where one could buy some food, and also Tombola clubs.

One such place called the Holiday Inn was very popular with servicemen. It had a stage as well as Tombola where sometimes someone might give a song. Where I used to go a lot to eat was a large restaurant called 'Firpos', the food being quite cheap. The officers frequented the Grand Hotel which was too posh for us. Very soon American soldiers appeared in the city, and while British troops had to be tidily dressed and keep upright because of the presence of Military Police, the Americans seem to loaf about more. I was to spend about eighteen months in Calcutta, so I got to know it quite well. About early June we moved from Barrackpore to a camp about five or six miles from Calcutta called Budge Budge, near the Hooghly river.

The camp was designated as 'Orange' site. It had four 3.7 inch mobile AA guns. The huts were brick with palm-leaf roofs, and the beds were called 'charpoys', being wooden frames, with coir matting tied to the top. We soon discovered that bedbugs were about the frame and matting. So we got rid of them by soaking the bed-frame and matting with paraffin which was plentiful. When you got out of bed in the morning, it was usual to turn your boots or shoes upside down, because you never knew what may be inside them. Sometimes kraits, which were small snakes no more than a foot long, got into your boot and even fell from the roof onto your bed. It was a very hot but humid atmosphere and we sweated quite a lot. The backs of our shirts being quite wet, when you dried them in the sun the backs used to be white because of the salt loss from your body. We had to have a mug with us on parade most mornings and were given a spoonful of salt to drink in water. When we first arrived in India we all had prickly heat, which felt like broken glass on your hands, cause by the sun and sweat, but it soon goes when one gets acclimatised.

We had a concrete dugout for a Command Post where I was either on duty on top or on the telephone below. One day we had a visit from General Wavell. I was on the telephone that day. He talked to me and asked where I was from. I told him "Wales", and he said he knew quite a few Welsh friends. At a later date his daughter Felicity travelled in our aircraft. I don't know if she was shy, but she never spoke to us.

On one occasion I was on duty on top of the Command Post armed with a rifle, and about five o'clock in the morning, the weather was foul, and I was feeling ill, so I thought it very unlikely anyone would be around. So I went below in the dugout and lay down on a bench, and that particular time and morning the orderly officer did call, and caught me away from my post. I was placed under close arrest, that means I was escorted everywhere I went to. Later that morning I appeared before Captain Moulsdale. He reprimanded me and told me how serious it was to leave one's post. I had no excuse for what had occurred, so I was sentenced to fourteen days 'Pack Drill' which meant that I was kept busy all day doing every hard job, and in the evening at six o'clock I had to report to a sergeant. I had to wear full uniform and a full pack with a rifle, and not being very robust physically it was a heavy load. I then had to do an hour's non-stop drill, with my rifle on my left shoulder, as the time went on my left elbow was going numb and felt painful. I did have feelings of rebellion and felt like throwing my rifle on to the ground, but considered that a lot of my friends would be watching me, and I wanted to show that I could take it. One thing I did was, as I was walking away from the sergeant, I dropped my left arm and held my rifle with my right arm; this was brief but allowed me to flex my left arm once or twice.

We had a football ground in the camp. I was glad because I liked playing football and only about a fortnight after we came to 'Orange' site at Budge Budge we had a football match at about seven o'clock in the evening. I was playing and a lieutenant also played. About half an hour after we started playing, the officer, Lt. Mitchener, felt ill and was taken back to his quarters. He had heat stroke and, feeling very hot, he was put into a bath of cold water with, I think, may be ice. It was the wrong thing to do, and the officer, who came from Winchester and was only nineteen years old, died at one o'clock that night from pneumonia. We were all very sorry for what had happened.

Our presence on an AA site was necessary, as there was still a possibility of the Japs advancing into India. They held the whole of Burma, and held Akyab and the Arakan coast, not that far from Calcutta. So it was that in July we had a daylight raid on Calcutta about midday. There must have been about six hundred aircraft, they were quite visible with their silver bodies, and they dropped quite a few bombs, which gave us the opportunity to use our guns.

There was a road running parallel with the main road to Chowringhee. The RAF had about half a dozen Hurricanes there. From where they were they could see the Grand Hotel where all the officers drank and ate. On the other side of the road that we called the Red Road was a large open space called the 'maidan' that had a racecourse which was quite modern, and a few football pitches. It was only when I returned home in 1945 that I learnt that my cousin, twenty-one years old in the RAF and had been on day leave in the city during the daylight raid and was unfortunately killed.

I usually had one day off a week, and used to like to go to the races, and have a flutter. We could also go on weekend leave and spend the weekend on the racecourse itself. The WVS supplied us with beds and food. The first night I stayed the weekend I was with two other friends and after a short while, having decided to sleep in the open on a wooden charpoy, we found that the beds were occupied by bed bugs, so we picked up our blankets and went to sleep instead on the concrete floor of the race stand, on the second floor. I went to the races one day and only possessed about ten rupees, and had one bet on the Tote. I managed to win about fifty rupees. Most of the jockeys were British so the soldiers used to ask the jockeys what they fancied when they paraded.

I was a bit nervous catching a tram back to the city. I was the only white person on the tram and thought what if someone robbed me of my money. I was always pestered by beggars, and also offered a "nice girl, Sahib?" There was another Battery actually stationed on the racecourse itself, but they were not part of our Regiment. I thought if I wasn't on leave at the racecourse I could still phone them up and get the winners, they had 'scopes and could quite easily see the results on the winners' boards.

For about four hours in the middle of the day no one worked because it was too hot. Some, of course, lay on their beds with only a towel over them, but a lot just hung around so I had the idea to operate a means of having a gamble. I took the table tennis top and placed it upright in the open, and purchased the morning paper off the cogage wallah (paperboy) in the morning. I was then able to chalk the runners for every race on the board, rubbing them off the board after a race. I managed to make paper strips that were numbered for every runner and when someone bet on a horse I gave him the number and put a chalk stroke beside the horse on the board. After the race I calculated the total number of tickets sold, and divided it by the number of winning tickets. It became so popular that the officers muscled in on it, and suggested I take a percentage out of the winnings to give towards the sports fund. I couldn't very well refuse. One Saturday two of the officers, Lt. Ellis and Lt. Pearce, said they were going to the races and asked if I could give them some winners. I gave them two horses and found out that they had won, so when I asked them if they had backed them they said no, because the tote queue was too long.

I never had anything to do with the guns, except paint a name on each gun for the boys, but one day during the midday break I was asked to give the guns a wipe down so I went up to the gun pit of one and heard a hissing and heavy breathing. I thought, 'What the hell is that?' I wasn't certain where the sound was actually coming from; there were four caissons, concrete bunkers with two thick doors around the gun pit and built up with earth between. I was puzzled because I could still hear the sound. I had to get some oily rags which I knew were kept inside along with the shells. I saw a wooden box with some rags in it so put my hand in, and found a snake inside with a frog in its jaws. I thought I was lucky that the snake's mouth was full! I then had to think what I should do next. I managed to find a long stick, and prudently stood on top of the caisson, and poked into the box and managed to kill it; it was about three feet long. I don't know what type of snake it was.

We were entertained one evening by one of the natives who had a basket of snakes. He ended his act by biting the live snake's head off and spitting it out. I should tell you that if bitten by a snake and there were six punctures from the bite, that is two rows of three punctures, it was safe but if you had two punctures it was poisonous, because the poison was injected into the victim through the two fangs.

Some of the men had all kinds of ailments. One of the soldiers in our tent should never have been abroad, he was gone forty-five years of age, and went missing for two days. He went wandering in the wilds and some natives found him and brought him back to camp. His clothes were all torn and he had lost his senses. He was shipped back home.

Our first Christmas overseas arrived and I made my own cards to send home by folding some cartridge-paper and painting some scenes in water-colour on them. Of course, some of the boys asked me to do some for them. On Christmas Eve we were in our hut and the only light we had was from paraffin lamps we made ourselves. We had no drink to celebrate with, so one of the boys went down to the village which was nothing more than a few mud huts. He came back with a bottle of something that looked like gin, anyway we drank it, and next morning I felt really terrible. I tried drinking plenty of water but it made me worse. I could not eat any breakfast and also missed my Christmas dinner, so I had a lousy Christmas.

Myself and about a dozen others were given a week's leave in Darjeeling, up near Nepal. I travelled by train to a place called Siliguri, which was the end of the main line and on the Nepal border. It was a journey of a couple of hundred miles. The scenery was spectacular with the line crossing some very big rivers. There were some really long rail bridges with not even a hand rail on either side, so when you looked down out of the window all you could see was the ground far below. At Siliguri we transferred to a narrow gauge railway, the Darjeeling Himalayan line. The coaches were wooden and very narrow, there was very little space to stretch out. There was an engine in the front and the back of the train and about four coaches, and a man would be on the front of each engine whose job was to rake out the ashes as the train was moving, because they used so much coal. The first stop we had was Kurseong, and then Kalimpong. The trip would take about six hours. Very soon we would be able to look down from a great height at the Indian plain in the distance. The train would circle over the line you had just been on and also switch back: going forward, stopping and then reversing to a higher level, then forward to a higher level again. They did this a few times, for it was the only way to climb such rocky and steep mountains. Frankly the ride was quite scary in parts. There were a lot of tea plantations on the way.

We finally arrived at Darjeeling and put up at a large house, where we had a great view of the snow capped Himalayan mountains with Mt. Kangchenjunga right in front of us. It is, I think, about 27,000 ft high. We found the people very friendly, and liked to walk around the market place. The most popular thing to buy was a kukri, a short broad-bladed sword, that the Gurkhas used in battle. There was a football pitch that had a sheer drop on three sides of it and, of course, a high fencing around it, and there was a club to go to in the evening where one could have a cup of tea or a drink. The permanent staff at the holiday centre usually had a whist-drive every evening, not very exciting. To see Mount Everest I would have had to get up at five in the morning and travel on horseback for fifteen miles. Then, when you reached a viewing point, you might see Everest covered in mist, and so not be able to see its peak. When I went out in the evening I usually dined at a Chinese place. We had a nice holiday.

A remarkable coincidence occurred one day when I missed the truck from Barrackpore to Calcutta. The only option I had was to go down to the main road into the city and hope for a lift, and much to my surprise a car stopped. I was thinking of a lift in a lorry but the driver of the car was white, which in itself was unusual. He was dressed in civvies and he asked me if I was going to Calcutta. I told him yes, and he asked me where my home was in Britain. I said South Wales. "Oh," he said, "I used to go to a town called Aberdare on business." I told him I was from Aberdare, and he said he used to go for lunch and a drink to a pub called the 'Britannia'. The pub he mentioned was a hundred yards from my home. I thought of the expression "It's a small world".

The Japs were still holding Akyab and the Arakan area. In February 1943, Orde Wingate made his first expedition behind the Jap lines in Burma. They cut various lines of Jap communication but achieved very little. His men were called Chindits.

They managed to extricate themselves, but had heavy casualties on the way back to India. About seven hundred or more men were lost, and our Regiment was still in Calcutta.

I had a week's leave and travelled by train to Tatanagar in Jamshedpur about a hundred and fifty miles away. The lady who met me on the train when I was on my way from Bombay to Calcutta had invited me to visit them if I wished. So it was a nice break that I could get away from the army for a while. They had a nice home with a couple of native servants, and they also had a daughter named Lorna; their surname, by the way, was Jones. They had a

With George Hartly in Calcutta, 1942.

Calcutta, 1943.

(Top)   Gulmarg, Kashmir.

(Middle) With my cousin Ossie on my return from the Far East, 1945.

(Bottom) The anniversary of VJ Day, 1995.

nice club, where everything was put on the bill. I played billiards with Mr Jones and every evening they had an open-air dance floor with all coloured lanterns. I always danced with Mrs Jones. They had very kindly written to my parents to say that I was all right.

We had our second monsoon in May. In the dry season the ground is burnt and very dry with no water anywhere, then when the monsoon starts it pours down for weeks, and streams form and even fish can be seen. It also drives the snakes from their nests in the ground.

One day I was on my way up to the Command Post and saw a python on the wet ground. It was about fifteen feet in length. I got hold of a long stick and killed it, I had no wish to see it hanging around. When the rain poured down some of the men stood outside naked with a piece of soap, and let the water run from the roof over them. About a quarter of a mile from our camp was a jute mill and we used to walk there to have a hot shower, since in our camp we only had cold water. Sometimes we would see a baboon; we avoided them because they could give you a nasty bite, and we used to have wild pariah dogs roaming the camp. Two men were usually detailed to take a rifle and shoot them, while the rest of the men kept inside out of harm's way, as some of the bullets used to ricochet off the hut walls. I used to run a few miles some mornings before breakfast for exercise, and we would play soccer in the evenings with a match sometimes against a native team who wore no boots but only ankle socks. I usually wore light leather boots.

There was a square-shaped water tank about eighty yards long, where we were able to have a bathe near the camp. In fact, I taught myself to swim in this tank. I dived in one day and caught my elbow on a rock, good job it wasn't my head!

There were quite a few natives working on the camp: the dhobi wallah laundered our clothes, the durzi wallah doing our tailoring, cutting or altering our clothes, the char wallah supplied us with tea which was stewed, and the corn wallah removed the corns on one's feet. They only had a horn about two inches long and about half an inch in diameter which tapered to a small hole at one end. With a ball of gum or gutta percha on the end, they placed the horn over the corn and sucked out the air and sealed it in one movement, creating a vacuum which drew the corn out. It was crude and painful.

Fruit was plentiful. We ate bananas, or plantains is what they really were, there being very little difference in looks or taste. Our food was monotonous. The bread was soggy, neither white or brown but an oily colour, if you rolled some up into a ball you could bounce it on the floor. Our meat was probably indian buffalo meat, it was very tough. Sometimes the potatoes were boiled in their jackets so we had to peel them on our plates which were made of tin. We cleaned our plates with cold water and sand. We usually had dinner about six at night and had tiffin, a light meal, about twelve o'clock. We never had eggs on the menu. Sometimes the natives supplied us in the evening with an egg and a piece of bread. The cookhouse was primitive, and I forgot to mention that the bread had quite a lot of weevils in it. We made it more likeable when the cook allowed us to toast it before we ate it.

We had a new officer about this time, at twenty-two about my age, Lt. Michael Robinson. When I was on duty on the telephone, I would take messages to him, and in the evening, he talked to me about his home in Argentina, and showed me photographs of his father's ranch. The officers were more lonely than us, we always had plenty of company off duty. There were about fifteen Welsh soldiers in our battery. I was always addressed as Taff or Taffy, only one other boy was called the same.

There was always someone sick at our camp in Budge Budge. Complaints were numerous such as ringworm, a red circle on one's belly as big as a dinner plate; Bengal Rot, when thanks to sweating a lot, it seemed that one's flesh was putrid between the toes and smelled awful.

Dysentery was also available, you could see the boys going back and forth to the latrines; jungle ulcers were also affecting some boys; one would have a sore about one inch long and a half inch wide and deep: it used to fester and felt very sore.

In early September 1943 I woke up one morning feeling terrible. I was so ill, I stayed in my bed, later I began to feel pains in my legs and lower back. I was feverish and felt burning inside and cold outside. I had my blankets over me. I lay ill all day, too ill to bother with anyone, and no one worried about me, they probably thought I was off-duty and resting. Around teatime a good friend of mine, a Geordie named Johnny Gray, came off-duty and said to me, "Are you all right, Taff?" I told him I felt ill, so he went to get an orderly, who handed out tablets or bandages whenever you needed them. One could also obtain 'French letters' from him, although their main use was to cover the fuse cap on the 3.7 inch shells so as they wouldn't get damp. Anyway the orderly, also a Geordie named Charlie Wilson, who we knew only had one testicle, took my temperature with his thermometer and found my reading was a 104°. He went and told the officer I was very ill, and so, riding in the back of a lorry with a blanket over me, I was taken to Calcutta to a hospital called Saint Lorenzo. I believe it was a convent now used as a hospital, 47BGH.

Here the nurse took a blood sample, and told me my temperature was 105°, and later next morning she told me I had contracted Dengue fever, a tropical disease that was apparently not uncommon in India. A boy in the bed next to me was moaning with pain a lot; he was only nineteen, I was twenty-three at that time early September 1943. I didn't see many nurses around, and one felt very isolated not being visited by anyone, but on the third day I felt a little better, and I struggled to get up out of bed. I managed to take a step but then fell down. I was put back into bed, and next day I was worse the fever having returned. I improved on the sixth day and was discharged on the tenth as fit for duty.

A lorry like a jeep picked me up next morning, to take me back to Orange site at Budge Budge. We had to go back through Calcutta so the driver said that as it was nearly lunchtime we could have a meal in Firpo's, so I agreed. I noticed that the wind was rising and leaves flying about with loose clouds in the sky. After the meal as we began to return to camp, we had only travelled a few miles when it began to get very rough with rain falling, and the sky was very dark. The wind was very strong and branches and debris were flying about, and making it difficult to drive, even with the windscreen wiper working overtime. It was difficult to understand how quick the storm engulfed us, although of course we were travelling into it. We had travelled about eight miles when we found a tree fallen on to the road. The driver and I decided that we had no choice but to walk the next few miles back to camp, though we were only wearing a khaki drill shirt and slacks. We were absolutely soaked and struggled against the force of the wind, and next day we learnt that we had run into a cyclone.

We finally managed to reach the camp, with no one at the entrance the whole camp under a foot of water. I waded to my hut, and found my bed was only a few inches above the water. I did not know what to do as the camp was deserted. I had no alternative but to lie on the bed; I was shivering with the wet and cold clothes on me. I was still puzzled as to where everyone had gone, when an officer poked his head into the hut and asked me why I wasn't up helping the other men. I told him I had just returned from hospital and knew nothing. He told me the river had overflowed and was the cause of the camp being flooded; he didn't say any more, so I lay back on my bed. He referred to the fact that the river Hooghly, a very large river, was in flood because of the cyclone, and the men were all sand-bagging and trying to stem the flood waters. I was soon asleep, hoping I wouldn't drown in my sleep. The storm had subsided by the next day, and the water soon flowed away, and there were snakes swimming around in the water amongst a lot of floating debris. Maybe I should have stayed in hospital a few more days.

Our unit went with our four AA guns to Jamshedpur for firing practice. It was a few hundred miles travelling and I sat in the back near the tailboard of the lorry. It was very warm and dusty and in the evening one side of my face was swollen and very painful, caused by the wind blowing in my face by the tailgate. I vowed never to do it again. We stopped and made camp in an orange grove, and the cooks rousted up some grub. I was thirsty and starving, but was in too much pain to eat or drink. Someone said I had caught 'blast'; it was something I imagined like neuralgia. We spent the night there but I didn't sleep much, somehow I had the knack for always doing the wrong thing! On reflection I think I was young and wild.

Next day we arrived by coincidence at Tatanagar where my Welsh friends were living. We had firing practice all at ground level, firing at some rocky hills in the distance, and we stayed in large tents. I was only able to see the Jones family once, my officer having granted me an evening off to see them. I travelled on my own walking to my friends' house. I noticed the air was filled with perfume from the jasmine. One felt like putting it into a bottle. I was made very welcome by my friends, who were surprised to see me; at dinner there was an officer present, he must have been friendly with Lorna the daughter. He asked me if I liked the army. I said sometimes I did and sometimes I didn't; this didn't please him, and he said that I and others had never had it so good. A few more words were exchanged and our host asked us to please eat dinner. Anyway, I had the most enjoyable evening, and the officer, whom I had not met previously, gave me a lift back to my camp.

When I entered my tent I could see it was empty and wondered where my fellow soldiers were, one of them then came in and said they were all down by the wire fencing that was around the camp being entertained by some wandering gypsies. One has to use one's imagination to know what kind of entertainment they were receiving. I never bothered to take a look.

In October 1943 Lord Mountbatten arrived in the Far East, making his HQ at Kandy in Ceylon, then designated SEAC. 11th Army Group was formed under General Gifford, and the Fourth Army under General Slim was under his command. About this time preparations were being made for the eventual return to Burma. The second return of the Chindits was to take place in February under Wingate. Our regiment, the 95th H.A.A. Regt. was to be disbanded, casualties had taken their toll in the Arakan and replacements had to be found. We were all given the choice of transferring to the Military Police (M.P.'s) – Movement Control – or to the Royal Signals. One tended to have a certain liking or dislike to the army among one's friends, and my friends had decided to transfer to the Royal Signals, so I also did the same. Next day we said goodbye to those who were leaving us, including our officers. Transport then took us to Howrah Station, the main railway station in Calcutta. It had the usual quota of beggars asking for "Buckshees Sahib". Some of the younger beggars were no more than about ten years old, and some would contort their arms and legs to appear disabled, hoping we would take pity and give them a few annas. Our destination was to be Mhow in north-west India, about two hundred miles north-east of Bombay and south of the Vindayha Mountains. Mhow was directly about eight hundred miles due west of Calcutta. The journey was the usual third class wooden carriage, and we were pestered by ants by day and cockroaches by night, and so we arrived at Mhow.

It was a very large military barracks; soldiers had used the camp since 1890. There was an outdoor bathing pool with seating all around it. It had an outdoor dance floor where an instructor would teach those who wished to dance. The day after we arrived we were told to go to a building where we were put into a kind of classroom. A colonel then addressed us and put certain questions to us. He told us that we were to train as cipher operators, and so began a couple of months of learning codes and how they operated, from book ciphers to machines. We had occasional exams to see how we were progressing. We were taught to never start a message at the beginning but choose anywhere after about five or six words. We also used padding, that is perhaps putting part of a nursery rhyme or well-known saying before and after a message. We were taught basic book ciphers, each of us were given a book about the size of a ledger with a code word of five letters for every word. Later we learned how to use a one day pad, which could not be broken because it was only used one day, a key word being necessary, of course, to decipher and encipher a message.

We were told one day that we would learn to touch-type, that is to type without looking at the keyboard. I thought to myself that I'll never be able to do that, but I did learn, and also became quite good at it. What they did was put a piece of card with the keyboard printed on it and put it above the actual keyboard in front of you, so you only looked at the card. You then placed the finger of the left hand on the first four keys of the centre row, and your right fingers on the last four keys of the centre row, the two centre keys being touched by the left thumb and right thumb; you then moved your fingers up to the top row of keys or down to the bottom row of keys, looking at the card all the time and pressing the key that you knew the position of by the top card in front of you. The aim was that once you knew the position of the keyboard letters you would not need the card. After a few months we had an exam but we were not told the result of the exam.

I was told that I would be transferred to 11th Army Group HQ in Kandy, Ceylon. So myself and about fifteen other soldiers travelled from Mhow to Kandy on about 19th of April 1944. It was a long journey and arriving at Madras, we were told it would be a few days before we could have the next train to Ceylon. We discovered a Salvation Army place there where we could have a bite to eat, and a bed. It was the first and last time I saw the Salvation Army in the Far East. We travelled to Colombo in Ceylon, and then by train to Kandy. It was a stiff climb but the view was quite good, passing tea plantations and rubber trees. We saw Pikes Peak, the highest point in Ceylon, and we learnt later that there were wireless transmitters on the Peak, with direct contact with London.

Kandy is a small town with a large lake. There was a fairly big hotel that was only used by officers; we could not afford to go there. Our camp was a few miles from Kandy and was new, the offices were close to our quarters which meant we didn't have far to walk. An officer introduced us to our work at the camp which was deciphering and enciphering messages; there were a few machines that we called 'Type X' machines, the machine had a typewriter keyboard and a drum each side, and beneath the keyboard were five wheels with cogs that made it resemble a bicycle chain wheel. On each wheel was every letter that was on the keyboard. The drum moved two tapes, one was plain English which went into one of the side drums, the other was encoded into five letter groups which went into the other side drum. If you typed the encoded letter groups you would get plain English letters and vice versa. Every message that left our cipher office went out in code, the tape with the encoded five letter groups being pasted onto plain paper then transmitted.

We used a different key word every day which we set on the five cogged wheels. Usually two men would be on the machine, and two men would be on book ciphers. Book ciphers were used at Division level; talking about Divisions I think I should mention that when I was posted to Kandy my best friend Johnny Gray was posted to the Chindits. I considered I was lucky to have a softer option. Next to the Cipher Office was a wireless room with transmitters using teleprinters; there was a hatch between the two offices where messages were exchanged for either transmission or deciphering. When the coded message was taken from the drum on the Type X machine it was stuck on to a plain piece of paper and passed through the hatch for transmission. The persons working there, including officers, were not allowed in the cipher room. There was always an officer on duty in the cipher room; by the way, I had been promoted to Corporal on first day at the office. When we received a coded message it would be classified immediate, secret, top secret, etc. The top classification was AG.AG, which would only be seen by the decipher clerk and the officer on duty. Every morning incoming messages from the day previous were put into a large oil drum and burnt, then pounded to dust.

When walking to our office or returning, we always used to see a few elephants with their mahouts. They were used mainly for hauling trees about.

I had a look around Kandy on my first day off-duty, looking around the few shops there, which often had Portuguese names like Da Silva, a reminder of past invaders of Ceylon. I visited the Temple of the Tooth, removing my shoes first of course; it was supposed to be a tooth of a tiger that Gautama Buddha had slain.

There were a lot of Buddhist monks about, easily noticeable because of their saffron or orangey-yellow robes, and they all had shaven heads. I saw quite a few parades by them through Kandy, with elephants fully adorned and fire-eaters shooting flames from their mouths. This was done by taking a mouthful of paraffin, blowing it out and lighting it with a firebrand they carried. Sometimes when I had a day off, myself and one or two others would get a packed lunch and walk about three or four miles to a place called Teldenaya, which had a sandy riverbank where we could lie in the sun and bathe in the small river; the other attraction was precious stones which Ceylon is well known for. I used to pick up handfuls of sand in the river, and sometimes find bits of ruby and, if lucky, bits of sapphire. We often used to take the stones to one of the merchants in Kandy, who would make us a ring with the stones placed on it. Another day off trip I used to take was to travel to Colombo, and go a couple of miles to a beach called Mt. Lavinia which had good sands and a nice bathing pool. Just off the beach coconuts and pineapples were plentiful as well as other fruits. One day I was with another friend on the beach and decided to go in the sea for a dip. I only swam about five yards and I could feel myself being dragged out to sea. I started swimming back to shore but found myself standing still. I could swim but I was not a powerful swimmer. I started to swim faster and faster and finally made the shore exhausted and glad to be back on dry land. If I had not been able to beat the undertow I would have drowned. The only help about was my friend and a woman selling pineapples.

Another day, I was with a soldier whom I knew but was not one of my friends, and we visited the Galle Face Hotel – a large posh hotel. I left my jacket which contained about fifteen rupees in the changing room. I asked one of the people working there if my clothes would be all right. He said yes, so I went for my swim, but when I returned to the changing room I found the money was missing from my wallet. I talked to the native attendants but they said they had not taken the money. Later I did remember that while I was in the water, my friend said he was going back to the changing rooms to get something. I am convinced that my money had been taken by the soldier I was with. I could not accuse him without proof, but one thing I did know was that he liked to visit certain ladies. I won't mention his name except he came from the Midlands.

One evening during my stay in Ceylon, I returned to my hut from the cipher office. Beside my bed I had a wooden chest and in one corner was a small wooden tray where I kept small knickknacks like pins and I knew where everything in the tray was. I needed something from the tray, I don't remember what, but I lifted the lid with my left hand and, without looking, put my right hand into the tray. I felt something like a needle stick into my finger. I looked down and saw a sand-coloured scorpion in the tray, stinging me. That was its last act. I felt slightly anxious about the poison it must have injected into my finger. Some of the other boys said I'd better go and see the orderly. I went to see him, and he told me he had no antidote, all I could do was sit it out for a while and come back to him if I became ill. I spent a few days of apprehension. On the tenth day I had a sore on my chest which began festering. It was about an inch long, half an inch wide and very deep. The medical orderly told me that it was probably the poison from the scorpion working its way out of my body.

On the 11th of November 1944, we were told we would be travelling to Barrackpore near Calcutta, where I had recently spent about eighteen months. After another long train ride we reached Calcutta and on to Barrackpore, where we set up a cipher section. It had an airstrip also, and on the 13th November Lt.-Gen. Sir Oliver Leese travelled to Barrackpore from Mountbatten HQ at SACSEA Kandy. There was some acrimony between Leese and Mountbatten. Leese being C-in-C ALFSEA – Allied Land Forces South East Asia, he had brought some of his senior officers from the Middle East to the Far East. This was not liked by some of the officers who had been some time in the Far East.

Mountbatten visited us one day, he said a few words to me; he was dressed in a smart light khaki uniform. Plans were already under way for a push back to Burma, Leese's aim being to reach Rangoon by the end of the monsoon season in May.

At this time I had a pleasant visitor. I was in Calcutta with another friend on leave, and in the evening I was in the Holiday Inn on Chowringhee having a cup of tea. An occasional singer got up on to the stage to give a song. I heard a voice from the stage shout, "Is Cpl Norman Boulton here?" I looked at the stage but could see no one I knew. I then walked to the stage and asked the man who wanted me. He said, "Oh, he's just gone by there." I looked and was surprised and happy to see my younger brother who was serving as a marine on the cruiser Newcastle. They had been busy shelling the coast of Sumatra. It was very unlikely that a cruiser would venture up the Hooghly river to Calcutta, but it had happened. He had spent all day looking for me. He knew from my letters that I was in Barrackpore so he travelled there first, only to find I was on leave that afternoon. The Holiday Inn was his last chance of seeing me, so it was lucky I was there. I arranged to meet my brother Haydn the next day, and I applied for four days leave, which was granted. We drank a lot of rum and gin those four days. On the last day he told me they were going home to the UK after he left me. I had a little cry to myself. I thought my brother is going home and I will still be here in the Far East.

We were fairly busy at the Cipher Office. We received 'Sitreps' – Situation Reports – every day from Divisions HQ's. These were usually very lengthy, and not every message received was word-perfect; the sender made errors with letters missing from words. These we called corruptions, and when we deciphered a message we would write the message with our opinion of what the corrupted word should be. Sometimes a couple of letters would be missing from one word and a lot of words would be wrong in a single message. In early 1945, General Leese was doing a lot of flying around Burma, India and, sometimes, China.

Being now very good at cipher operations, I was asked by my officer, Captain Stirret, if I would go on flights on General Leese's communication aircraft. I didn't have to go, but I agreed. The General's plane was a Dakota Douglas DCII, a very reliable aircraft, he had the words Holly Cholly painted on the nose of the plane. My plane was also a Dakota, with Hermes on the nose, and everywhere that General Leese travelled, we would accompany him in our plane, so that when we landed somewhere we could communicate with our HQ or elsewhere.

The first time I flew, I and another cipher operator and an officer were told what time to report to Barrackpore airstrip. When we arrived the plane was on the airstrip. I had never flown before so I was a bit apprehensive about it all. Anyway an American jeep turned up with two flying officers and a navigator who was a sergeant. They didn't waste much time, they got on board and told us, "Okay, hop on board!" and off we went, I was on my first flying experience. I forget where we went to on that first flight, it was somewhere in northern Burma. When we put down at an airfield the two flying officers would be off somewhere without a word. Only the sergeant navigator would have any conversation with us. We had our own wireless operator also on flights with us; our first aircraft, a Dakota, was pretty bare inside with a long canvas seat running the length of the plane on each side. There were a few parachutes above us, on the rack, and we would be looking at them and hoping we would not need them; we would not know how to use them anyway. I soon got quite used to flying. After a few flights we had a better Dakota with forward-looking seats that were quite comfortable. I remember on one flight we had a passenger that happened to be General Wavell's daughter.

In April we had a sweep, the winner being the man who forecast the date of the D Day invasion of the French coast. We knew it was imminent soon.

In the space of a few months General Leese flew over 35,000 miles. I was to spend a total of eighty hours flying time with him. One flight took us about ten hours, stopping at Delhi around midday, where we had great difficulty getting a meal at an American mess hall at the airport. Once it's past mealtime the Yanks served no one. In the British army the cooks moan to latecomers but they do give you a meal.

There was a top-level meeting there at Delhi, because I recognised some of the aircraft on the airfield, one in particular being General Dan Sultan's. He was the American C-in-C and his plane had the logo on its nose, 'Dan Sultan's Magic Carpet'. We then flew on to Quetta on the Northwest Frontier of India, which is now Pakistan. Quetta is the Staff college where General Leese was previously Chief Instructor, it was situated on the northern border of Baluchistan. Then we went on to Peshawar further north-east on the Afghan Border. There was an RAF base there so we were all right for accommodation. The local RAF bases seemed far away from the war in Burma. As we wore green denims and Bush hats, they told us not to wander too far from the airfield; some of the locals occasionally threw a couple of hand grenades over the fence. We could have bunked with the RAF but preferred to sleep in our aircraft. We could see the well known Khyber Pass from the airfield, and also had a view of Mount Godwin Austen (K2) in the distance.

On the return flight to Calcutta we passed over the Taj Mahal at Agra. On our return from another flight, when I landed my Captain said, "Everything okay, Sergeant?" and he told me I had been promoted to Sergeant. On some of my flights I had an RAF crew on the plane, they were more particular than the Yanks about giving the plane a good once-over before take off, not like the Yanks who were up and away at once. The Yanks always had plenty of K Rations on board, a carton about ten inches long, four inches wide and about two inches deep. Inside were biscuits, a piece of chocolate, a tin of Spam, three cigarettes and even a piece of toilet paper.

Our offensive in Burma was going well now, we had surprised the Japs by taking the offensive during the monsoon season, when one was more often wet than dry. With plenty of rain around, Meiktila, a main Japanese base for air attacks on India and the Arakan in Burma, was taken by our troops on 5th March 1945, with Mandalay falling on the 20th. I was to visit both at a later date. I managed to get a few days off in Calcutta, which was now filled with American armaments on all open spaces. I was having a meal at Firpo's on Chowringhee one evening, and was surprised to see my good Geordie friend Johnny Gray, whom I mentioned earlier had gone to the Chindits. They had made a second operation about February into Burma. He told me he had a very rough time and was glad to survive. He said they were attacked a lot by Jap planes. He told me he was with a West African Battalion, who were all right in daytime, but at night they fired at anything that moved, sometimes their own men as they were very jittery in the dark.

I was doing a lot of flying at this time, one flight we took was to northern Burma to Bhamo at the top end of the Burma Road. It was on the Chinese border and we flew over some mountains to get there. General Dan Sultan, an American, was commander of the area – N.C.A.C. Northern Combat Area Command. The 36th British Division was attached to this command. The camp at Bhamo was entirely American, and we had good food for the time we spent there. In the American army everyone queued for meals, be they OR's, NCO's and officers. We were able to watch a film on the evening of our arrival there. They fixed up a screen in the open, but I don't remember what film it was. The next morning we had a good breakfast of bacon, beans, etc. and a flapjack which was common at American breakfasts, with treacle poured over it all. I was pro-American but I think I was biased in that direction because I had a cousin who was a Major in the American forces, and served in Japan after the war.

We took one flight to Bangalore in southern India. I knew about the Mosquito two-engined fighter, so I was pleased to see one on the airfield. I was on duty on the aircraft Hermes, with an Indian driver and his lorry in attendance. I was told that there was an RAF canteen just off the airfield, so I asked him if he would take me there in his vehicle, he refused so I said if he would lend me his lorry I would drive there myself. After a lot of persuasion he loaned me the lorry, and on my way back I had to drive amongst aircraft when something distracted my attention for a moment. When I looked up I could see the wings of an aircraft coming straight towards me. I instinctively ducked and just scraped under the wings of the plane. I shudder to think of my fate if I had knocked the aircraft.

On May the 8th we travelled to Akyab on the Arakan coast. We went to see the Divisional HQ, and had a chat with the cipher operators there; they only looked about nineteen years old, and I asked one of them if I could type one of his messages for him. It was meant for our HQ at Barrackpore, and I also knew that the operators knew that I had gone to Akyab so I inserted a few words of my own at the end of the message. When I returned to my HQ one of the boys said they had recognised my message.

We then travelled on to Mandalay and flying over it we could look down on the hill where some dead Japs were still lying. Just after we left Mandalay behind we flew into a tropical storm. That was not unusual in the area and, being the end of the monsoon season with thunder and lightning flashing around us and heavy rain, with the plane dropping suddenly at times, I was very sick. I had been seasick, now I was airsick: I staggered somehow to the rear of the plane to the toilet, where I emptied my stomach. After a while we flew out of the storm and landed at Meiktila. We arrived there in the evening. Some time later on the 8th of May, we heard on the radio that the war in Europe had ended, which made us wonder when our war would end. We slept the night on the ground under the aircraft wings.

Next morning, we could se a bulldozer at work, and wandered over to see that the bulldozer was clearing up dead Japs pushing the bodies into trenches. There were dead Japs all around the airstrips with spare limbs here and there. I don't think Japs are very nice looking alive, but they look a lot worse dead. During the morning the Yanks managed to get hold of a vehicle so we thought we would go to the big lake that was not too far away. We drove through the town, which was heavily damaged, and getting stuck in the mud at times. It was the rainy season, and when we got to the lake, we thought we might have a swim in the lake.

Being in a warm country we always had a dip at the first opportunity, but here we only went into the water a few yards, and soon came back out. There were parts of Japanese bodies in the water, and all around the lake was littered with dead Japs, trenches, shell cases and the usual battle debris. Meiktila was the Japs main base for supply to the Japanese troops facing the British. They also used the airstrip a lot for their airstrikes, so they put up a hard fight for it. Only when I returned home did I learn that my cousin was in the fighting at Meiktila; he was in the 17th Indian Div., and he lived opposite me back home.

I believe General Leese went to Meiktila to see General Slim, as changes were taking place at a top level of Command. Leese did in fact go to see Slim at Meiktila. General Slim was commander of the IVth Army, and Leese informed him that he was to be relieved of his command and given the lesser task of mopping up in Burma. This Slim refused to accept seeing it as the sack. When news got out about Slim's dismissal, the IVth Army was in a state of rebellion; officers and men. Leese himself was dismissed, and his place as C-in-C Allied Land Forces South East Asia taken over by Slim. Slim had gone to see Churchill back home and it was he who had appointed Slim.

Leaving Meiktila we travelled to Rangoon which had fallen earlier. We landed at Mingaladon airfield, and were taken to be billeted a large house a few miles away on the edge of Victoria Lake, a quite large lake. We were myself, an RSM who was not a cipher officer but accompanied us, and the American pilots and navigator. We had two Burmese cooks, and ate nothing but green stuff for two days. We used to complain and call them stupid bastards with no affect; they only laughed and giggled. Not being able to speak English they thought they were being praised! The Yanks really got fed up, and one night took a rifle and shot someone's cow, so we then had meat for breakfast, dinner and tea.

By the way, someone was always on duty on the Hermes, our plane. Changing over on shifts, I managed to get to the centre of Rangoon city, which was badly damaged with piles of rubble everywhere. Japanese paper money was everywhere; the Japs had printed their own money which they used to purchase goods, but it was not worth a light. I saw the beautiful Golden Pagoda, a Buddhist temple that was known worldwide and the usual pagodas. Our house being by the lake, we had a few dips in it; we managed to find a boat like a skiff and rigged up a mast and a sail on it. We had a couple of pieces of wood for oars, and four of us ventured on to the lake which was about two miles long and about as wide. We seemed to be sailing nice and quickly. As usual I was the clever one, and thinking the boat wasn't going too fast, I dived overboard to have a swim. The next thing I knew the boat had gone away from me, leaving me stranded in the middle of the lake. None of the boys knew anything about sailing, so they could not turn the boat around. I looked to shore which seemed a long way off, but saw an island in the middle of the lake which looked a bit nearer, so I decided to make for it. I tried every swimming stroke I knew, and eventually made it to dry land. There was a large house on the island and my mind was filled with thoughts like, what if a Jap is hiding in the house, or any booby traps. I walked in a bathing costume to the house which seemed to be built of timber. Inside the walls of the largest room was showing Japanese posters, I had a good look around, then went out again. I could see my friends in the boat making some progress towards the island. They had managed to steer the boat around, and eventually they picked me up.

It was June 1945, there was a victory parade going through the city of Rangoon but I didn't see it because I was on duty on Mingaladon airfield on the Hermes. We were told to pick up an RSM and a sergeant the next day to take back to our plane, so myself and another sergeant drove in a jeep to pick them up. We knew we were half an hour late but thought, wrongly as it happened, that it would be all right. Instead we got into a hell of a row with the RSM, he was Scottish and we called him 'Bob'.

At this time, the war in Burma being over, thoughts were already being focused on Malaya. General Leese decided to have a holiday in Kashmir, so he went in Holly Cholly and we accompanied him in Hermes. The pilot told us that an aircraft the size of our Dakota had never landed on Srinagar airfield before. It was a spectacular flight through the mountains which were some of the highest in the world. We landed at Srinagar and found that little distance separated us from the end of the runway and a sheer drop. General Leese stayed at the Maharaja of Kashmir's Number One Guest House, and five of us stayed at the Number Two Guest House. It was a large house and outside were some large brown tents, very much like the tents you see in Arab films. Myself and another sergeant decided to sleep in the tents, which we thought would be cooler. There were two beds in the tent. Sometime during the night I opened my eyes and noticed that a pair of socks I had washed and hung on a guy rope in the opening were swinging back and forth. There was not a breath of wind and then the tent seemed to be moving slightly. It must have been an earth tremor which was quite common in that part of the world.

The view next morning was marvellous, with snow-capped mountains in the distance, one of which was Nanga Parbat. I had now seen three of the world's highest mountains. On our first day we went on a Shikari, a long boat which would hold two or three people and the rower. Sometimes there were two rowers in the boat. We were taken by boat up the River Jhelum which had numerous wooden bridges crossing the water here and there. Where we alighted to visit a native shop, there were lovely wooden carvings of elephants in teak, caskets, brasswork and coats of goat's hair. Also beautiful embroidered shawls, but unfortunately we did not have a lot of money to spend. Srinagar looked very much like Venice with its numerous waterways, some of which flowed into the Dal Lake which was very large. There was a wooden structure on the lake from where we could dive and have a swim. There was a lot of plants in the water but it never bothered us. The Kashmiris were not so handsome as some of the races in that part of the world, most of them tended to look a little scruffy. There were hundreds of houseboats on the waters of Srinagar and the neighbourhood.

We decided one day to visit Gulmarg. We had been told that at this altitude we would have a better view of Nanga Parbat. The altitude at Gulmarg was about eight thousand feet. Some of the other boys were not too keen to travel to Gulmarg, so eventually just myself and another sergeant decided to go. We hired a couple of ponies and rode to Gulmarg, the journey taking about two hours. Gulmarg was only a few scattered wooden buildings. We managed to find a place to have a bite to eat and a drink. To our surprise we were asked whether we would like some strawberries and cream. We said we would. Afterwards we rode to Tangmarg higher up where we were able to touch the snow at the snowline. Time was going on so we decided to make our return journey and we asked the pony man how much we owed him. We thought the price was high and told him so, arguing with him quite a lot, which only drew more Kashmiris. We were outnumbered and I thought discretion safer than valour so we paid up. I had no wish to be reported as missing.

A few days later we received a message 'for eyes only' which meant it had to be delivered to General Leese only. I was on duty so I had to take the very top secret message to the Number One Guest House. The door to the house was closed so I knocked and a captain came, probably his A.D.C. whom I did not know. He held out his hand but I told him I could only give it to the General. He went back inside and General Leese came out, I gave him the message and he asked me how I was enjoying myself in Kashmir. "Very well, thank you Sir," I said. "The only fault is we don't have much money." "That is the trouble," he said. He was spending his holiday mostly fishing.

Only later was I to learn that Mountbatten had dismissed my General. Leese's place was taken by General Slim, whom Leese had wanted to dismiss himself.

Even among Generals you have dog eat dog. I have often wondered if the secret letter I had handed General Leese had been the fateful letter. I will never know. Leese was easy to talk to, unlike some officers I had met.

One day we decided to visit the Shalimar Gardens. It was only a few miles away. It was historically famous, having been built by Shah Jahan for his wife Mumtaz Mahal. The gardens run miles down the mountainside into the Dal Lake, with little streams and pools all round, usually with stone beds. There were various terraces of trees in symmetrical order and flowers everywhere. It is difficult to describe how beautiful it was. One could also see water cascades which caused misty sprays. On the top terrace was a black pavilion. How beautiful the gardens must have looked in Shah Jahan's day.

Our visit to Kashmir coming to an end, we flew back to Calcutta on an eight hour flight. It was the end of July 1945, I was twenty-five years old and a little bit older and wiser than when I first travelled to the Far East. I knew that our war would end soon, but how soon I did not know. I considered that I had been lucky so far to survive. The dropping of the atom bombs on Japan in mid-August was the one thing that determined the end of the war.

I now began thinking of home, as I had been in the Far East for nearly four years. I decided that I wouldn't push my luck too far, and when I was asked to go on another flight, I apologised to my officer and requested that someone else take my place. He acceded to my request.

A few days thereafter, the war ended and Captain Stirret, my boss and a very nice officer, came to me at the Cipher Office and said, "Sergeant Boulton, how would you like to become a Field Marshall?" I looked at him and before I could reply, he said that the only thing is I would have to stay on a bit longer in the Far East. "I am recommending you for a commission."

I was certain that my parents would be looking forward to seeing me now that the war had ended. I thanked him for his consideration of me but had to decline his recommendation, probably if he'd asked before the war had ended I would have accepted.

We were now ordered to return to Ceylon, taking our Type X machines with us – we were carrying very hot property. We left Barrackpore for the last time and travelled to Howrah railway station where we demanded first class coaches, something you don't see a lot of on Indian trains. While we were standing on the platform a few officers tried to enter our coach but we told them we were carrying secret equipment. The didn't like it but they didn't force the issue. We arrived at Colombo after a few days tedious train journey. I had to leave some of my friends here and I went to a transit camp. After a few more days, I boarded the liner Queen of Bermuda, a sister ship of the liner I had travelled out on. It had taken me eight weeks to travel out to the Far East but it only took twenty-one days to return. I arrived in Southampton in early October and phoned my parents who arranged a party for my homecoming. I had to stay on board ship till next day so I missed my party.

After a few enjoyable weeks I returned to the army, staying at various camps in England. I was discharged on June 16th, 1946. My total war service being six years and five days.